BLOOMIN' TALES

LEGENDS OF SEVEN FAVORITE TEXAS WILDFLOWERS

Cherie Foster Colburn

Illustrations by **Joy Fisher Hein**

bright sky press
HOUSTON, TEXAS

bright sky press
HOUSTON, TEXAS

2365 Rice Boulevard, Suite 202,
Houston, Texas 77005

ISBN: 978-1-936474-18-9

10 9 8 7 6 5 4 3 2 1

Library of Congress Cataloging-in-Publication Data on file with publisher
Editorial Direction, Lucy Herring Chambers
Creative Direction, Ellen Peeples Cregan
Designer, Marla Garcia
Illustrations, Joy Fisher Hein
Printed in China by RR Donnelley

For my cherished grandchildren,
Seth, Willow, Morgan and Caelin

~ JFH

With appreciation and love:
to my Aunt Boo, Opal Lou Foster, who taught me to tell a story;
to naturalist and author, Zoe Merriman Kirkpatrick,
who taught me each wildflower has a story to tell;
and to my beautiful daughters, Emily Katherine and Sarah Brittany,
who taught me the story continues only if we continue to tell it.

~ CFC

TABLE OF CONTENTS

Bushy Fox's Tail

With every farmer in the land after his tail, Bushy Fox was tired of hiding. But hide he must, since the farmers believed a fox's tail to be a powerful good luck charm. So far, it had been a good luck charm for Bushy, for sure.

Each night he crept through the dark toward the chicken coop, hoping to sneak a few eggs from under the sleeping hens. And each night, he heard the farmer's sons out in the dark field. They waited for him, arguing who would capture the fox and take his fine, full, black-tipped tail to sell at the market.

Bushy turned back to his den dug into the soft earth near the grass field, his head low with disappointment, his tummy aching with hunger.

"You must go to King Reynard," said Mrs. Fox. "Without eggs, our pups will starve. The good king will help us."

The king of the foxes lived a day's journey from the grass field. How could Bushy find the strength for such a trip? He knew Mrs. Fox was right. He must ask for help. This was not something he could do on his own. Soon his young pups would be too weak to live.

The next night, Bushy Fox set out, creeping low where the lights of the houses shone brightly. He listened for voices, but the darkness was heavy with sleep. Soon Bushy's fear of being captured went away. He was moving at a trot when a light ahead of him glimmered slightly. What was it? Behind that tree… Was it a lantern? Could a farmer be ahead, laying a trap? Bushy froze. When the light flickered again, he realized it was not moving at all. The wind was forcing a low branch to sway in front of a lighted window. As Bushy hurried past the farmhouse, the sun began its own journey for the day. The sky was turning a soft peach color when Bushy neared the den of King Reynard.

No one guarded the den this early morning. Bushy went straight for the opening near a pile of rocks. The king himself was returning from a successful hunt, breakfast hanging from his mouth. "Join me, friend," said the king, dropping the food to the ground. Another fox picked it up and carried it inside the hole.

"What brings you so far from home?" the king asked Bushy.

"My family is starving, good king. I go out each night to the chicken coop to take eggs for my pups. The farmer's sons wait there for me, and last week I barely escaped with my life. I made it past their trap, but I woke one of the hens when I took her egg. She made a horrible noise. Soon the farmer's boys surrounded me. I ran between their legs, losing considerable fur on my side where one grabbed me.

"We must do something to help," the king told Bushy. "When the fairy people come out for the night, I will confer with them."

At nightfall, King Reynard came out of his den and barked softly at the dusky sky. In moments, tiny lights enveloped the fox king, pin-dots, darting in every direction. He told the fairies of Bushy's dilemma. They sparkled, and giggled, and sparkled more. They shot up, dove past the king and into a stand of pretty, cupped flowers nearby. When they returned to the king, the fairies had a solution to the problem. King Reynard thanked the fairies. He told Bushy the advice the fairies had gotten from the flowers and sent him on his way.

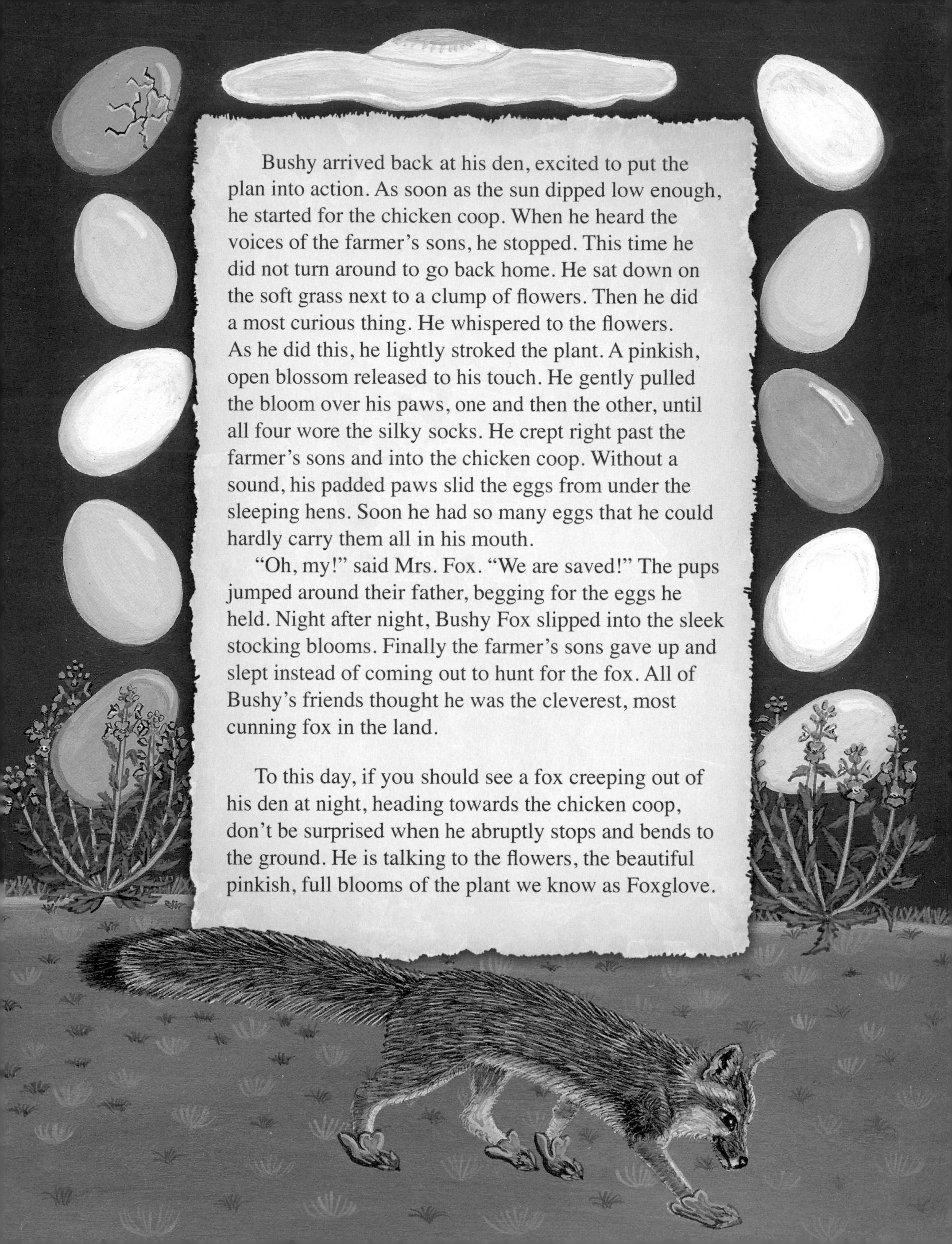

Bushy arrived back at his den, excited to put the plan into action. As soon as the sun dipped low enough, he started for the chicken coop. When he heard the voices of the farmer's sons, he stopped. This time he did not turn around to go back home. He sat down on the soft grass next to a clump of flowers. Then he did a most curious thing. He whispered to the flowers. As he did this, he lightly stroked the plant. A pinkish, open blossom released to his touch. He gently pulled the bloom over his paws, one and then the other, until all four wore the silky socks. He crept right past the farmer's sons and into the chicken coop. Without a sound, his padded paws slid the eggs from under the sleeping hens. Soon he had so many eggs that he could hardly carry them all in his mouth.

"Oh, my!" said Mrs. Fox. "We are saved!" The pups jumped around their father, begging for the eggs he held. Night after night, Bushy Fox slipped into the sleek stocking blooms. Finally the farmer's sons gave up and slept instead of coming out to hunt for the fox. All of Bushy's friends thought he was the cleverest, most cunning fox in the land.

To this day, if you should see a fox creeping out of his den at night, heading towards the chicken coop, don't be surprised when he abruptly stops and bends to the ground. He is talking to the flowers, the beautiful pinkish, full blooms of the plant we know as Foxglove.

Starry Dreams

Mesha lay on a big rock jutting out over the lake. His back soaked in the warmth of the stone. Heavy clouds from the morning's rain sailed further and further away, leaving only a soft blue in their wake. He stared into the sky until his eyelids grew heavy. When he could no longer keep his watch, Mesha, the son of a great chief, dreamed a great dream. In his dream, a young star came to him.

"Can you help me?" Young Star asked. "I want to live near the children, to hear their voices chant in harmony, to watch their strong tanned legs run and jump," she said. "The other stars in the night sky are ancient, existing long before man came to earth." Star told Mesha she felt alone, because the old stars had no patience for her questions or her energy.

Mesha felt sorry for Star. She was beautiful, her bright white light sparkling soft and clear. “The mountain might be a good place for you,” Mesha suggested. “From its peak you could see the whole village, and you would still be close to your home in the sky.”

Young Star agreed. She shot up the mountain and lit on the edge of the cliff, just above the village. Every day she looked down on the teepees, watching the comings and goings of the people until their fires grew dim. Day after day it was the same. Once a small child saw her shining on the mountaintop and tried to visit, but the steep mountainside was too difficult to climb. The wind whistled constantly, muting all the children’s happy voices.

Star again came to Mesha asking for help. "What will I do?" she asked. "I am so lonely. I suppose I must return home."

"The field is where we play each day. Come and live among the grasses and you will be near us," Mesha replied. So Young Star dove into the heart of the sweet prairie rose. The children romped around her, laughing and calling for her to watch them.

In time, bison returned to graze on the tall grass. The braves hunting the huge beasts forgot about the plants under their feet. They trampled the prairie rose that held Star. The dangerous hunting ground was no place for children, so she had no companions. Young Star was lonely and afraid. She decided she had no choice but to return to her home in the night sky.

Shooting up into the heavens, she glanced down for one last look at the earth she loved. A beautiful young star skimmed across the clear lake below her. Not realizing it was her own reflection, she floated back to the earth to meet this new friend who smiled at her from the lake. She landed silently on the water's smooth surface. Young Star knew that she was home.

Mesha awoke to find a full moon replacing the sun in the sky. His dream felt so real that now it seemed like the darkness was the dream. He sprinted back to the village to tell his father of his vision. Quietly approaching the chief who sat at the fire among his braves, Mesha waited anxiously for his father to look up at him. Then Mesha began his amazing tale. He proudly told his father how Young Star had chosen him to help her find a home.

The listening braves looked at one another, and they began to laugh. His father's mouth tightened. "Such an imagination could be better used in other ways, my son."

Mesha was crushed. He no longer felt like the great chief's son, but like an outcast. No one believed him. How could he blame them? He was not a seer for his people. It had just been a childish dream. Mesha shuffled toward the teepee of his family, his head low in shame. His face stung from the braves' laughter, but his father's disapproving words hurt most of all.

With the first light Mesha woke and began his chores. He was careful not to wake his father, afraid those dark eyes would still hold anger. When his chores were done, he trudged toward the lake to collect water for his sister. He was not anxious to return to the village. As he came upon the lake, he could not believe what he saw. An enchanting flower—a fragrant white lily—floated on the calm surface.

Mesha's vision was real. Young Star *had* chosen him to find her new home. He turned to go to his village, but others had already gathered at the water's edge. No longer laughing, now they smiled at him knowing he had brought this beautiful white star flower to them. And Mesha, the son of a great chief, saw his great dream come true.

You can still find the water lily on a summer morning floating on a quiet pond, her glowing white, star-shaped petals pointing up to her old home in the sky. Huge notched pads surround her like flowing hair, hiding a strong stem that holds her tight to her new home, the earth. She is often surrounded by others, all silent watchers, waiting for the children to return.

joy fisher hein

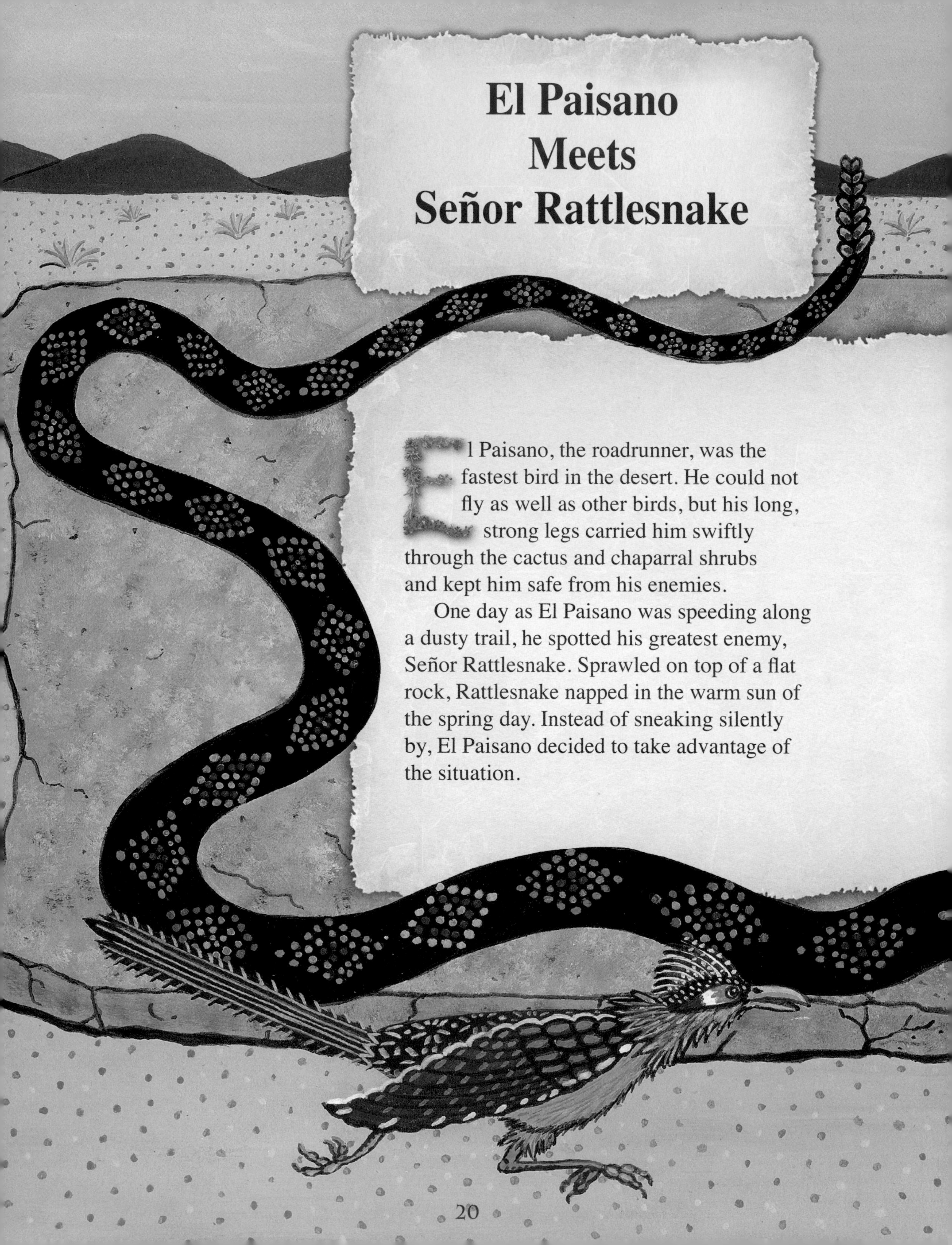

El Paisano Meets Señor Rattlesnake

El Paisano, the roadrunner, was the fastest bird in the desert. He could not fly as well as other birds, but his long, strong legs carried him swiftly through the cactus and chaparral shrubs and kept him safe from his enemies.

One day as El Paisano was speeding along a dusty trail, he spotted his greatest enemy, Señor Rattlesnake. Sprawled on top of a flat rock, Rattlesnake napped in the warm sun of the spring day. Instead of sneaking silently by, El Paisano decided to take advantage of the situation.

Remembering a plant he had dodged just before coming upon Señor Rattlesnake, El Paisano circled back, quickly finding the flash of yellow he'd seen perched on a fortress of needles. He carefully broke off pieces of the plant with his long beak. Placing them end-to-end, he worked with the thick, fleshy pads, cautious not to touch the sharp spines. Back and forth he went, from the spiky plant to the sleeping snake.

Before long, Señor Rattlesnake was surrounded with a fence too high to cross.

El Paisano stepped back to appreciate his work just as Señor Rattlesnake moved to sun a different part of his long body. But when Señor Rattlesnake stirred, he brushed against the spiny corral El Paisano had built to contain him. He felt a sharp jab of pain. How had this happened? He was a prisoner!

Señor Rattlesnake coiled his body tight, pointed his tail into the air and shook the rattles inside to sound the alarm. “Let me out of here, bird!” he hissed.

“Perhaps,” said El Paisano. “But first you must make a promise, Señor.”

“Never!” said Rattlesnake, and he rattled his tail again in anger.

“Then get used to your new home,” said El Paisano.

Señor Rattlesnake tried to move again. But each time he slithered right or left, a sharp needle pricked him. He stopped his struggle and glared at El Paisano. “Get me out of here, bird, or I will kill you!” said Señor Rattlesnake.

“First you must make a promise,” said El Paisano again.

After a long silence, Señor Rattlesnake realized he was at the mercy of El Paisano. "What is it you want, bird?"

El Paisano spread his broad tail feathers and fluffed the feather crown above his forehead. "Promise me you will never again hurt the babies of the desert. Whether they fly or crawl or run along the dusty trails like I do, no harm must come to them from your venomous bite. If you make me that promise, I will let you go. If you do not, you will die here in your prickly prison."

Señor Rattlesnake looked around. Without the help of this bird, there was no hope of escape. He knew what his answer must be.

Many days passed, and Señor Rattlesnake was hungry. He snacked on a couple of small spiders but that did not help. Then, he spied Little Jack Rabbit. Señor Rattlesnake became like a statue, motionless, watching the baby bunny from behind a bush. He twitched his eyes back and forth, looking for Mrs. Rabbit, but no one was in sight. Effortlessly, Señor Rattlesnake slid forward, positioning himself in front of Little Jack Rabbit. He began swaying his head, first to one side and then to the other, his tongue flicking in and out of his mouth. Little Jack was terrified. He knew he should hop away, but he was unable to move. Señor Rattlesnake had charmed him.

Just as Señor Rattlesnake crept closer to Little Jack, El Paisano came by to check on the Rabbit family. Rattlesnake was now near enough to strike the trembling bunny. Seeing a piece of the spiny plant that had earlier been Señor Rattlesnake's prison, El Paisano grabbed it with his beak and snuck around behind the snake. Just as Señor Rattlesnake opened his mouth to bite the little rabbit, El Paisano, quick as a lightning flash, sprinted forward and stuffed the thorny pad into the snake's mouth! Señor Rattlesnake could not move his mouth; it was stuck open, his pronged tongue caught by the sharp thorns of the prickly plant. Señor Rattlesnake slithered away, never again to harm anyone with his poisonous bite.

So watch for a sulfur yellow flower sitting on top of a cactus in the spring time. When the juicy red fruits replace the flower in summer, you might be tempted to pick the prickly pears. Instead, carefully peek beneath the plant. You might discover a little bunny playing there, safe under the arms of the Prickly Pear Cactus.

joy fisher hein

Frolicking Fairies

Some say fairies lived among us in days of old. Much like humans, the fairy children delighted in games. In sunny meadows, among the giant oaks of the forest, and on the lush hill-top you might find them choosing teams for red rover or tag. But on warm summer days, most likely you would spot them splashing in the cool water of the brook, or fashioning tiny mud pies along the water's edge.

One summer's morning, the fairy children rushed out into the new day, their wings fluttering wildly in anticipation of adventure. "Do not get dirty this morning," warned Mother Fairy. "The Dew Fairies just washed your clothes. They will be angry if they have to wash again so soon. And please stay away from the creek. Whenever you get near the water, you come home with mud from toe to wingtip. The creek is a dangerous place for fairies. Frogs and turtles lie in wait for a snack just your size!" The fairy children widened their eyes in mock fright, then they giggled and darted past Mother Fairy.

They started their games with a round of hide-and-seek in the woods. Behind knobby trees, in hollow logs and under piles of crumbling leaves, the fairy children hid, tucking their gossamer wings close beside them. The tall meadow grass whispered in the wind, beckoning them to the fragrant flowers further from home. Before they knew it, they found themselves at the brook's edge. Hot and dirty from their play, they flitted to the slippery rocks along the bank of the cool water.

"Stop!" Fairy Bright Eyes, the oldest of the fairy children reminded her eight brothers and seven sisters in her best big sister voice. "We promised we wouldn't get dirty."

"But we are already dirty," Fairy Freckles said. "Mother Fairy will be cross with us."

"We can wash out our clothes before anyone sees us. That way the Dew Fairies won't have extra washing to do and we won't be in trouble with Mother Fairy," said Fairy Curly Hair.

"What a wonderful plan!" they all agreed, their little wings flickering so fast they were almost invisible.

The fairy children scrubbed their teeny skirts, tiny frocks and wee pants against the rocks until they shined. Then they carefully laid them out to dry on a small clump of green, heart-shaped leaves. Suddenly a loud "RRRRRRIBIT!" followed by a big "SPLAAAAASH!" startled them. They scurried away as fast as their wings could carry them.

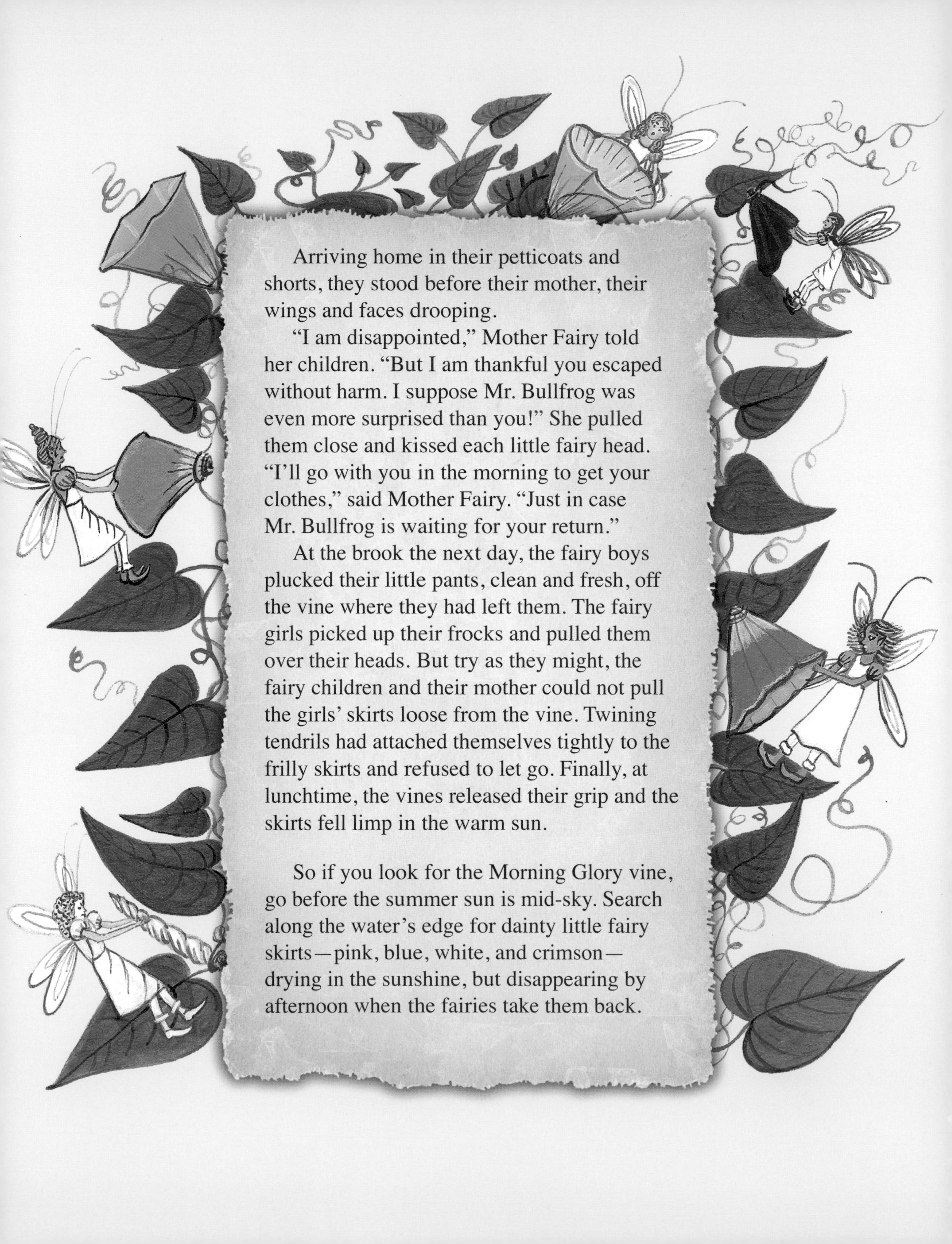

Arriving home in their petticoats and shorts, they stood before their mother, their wings and faces drooping.

"I am disappointed," Mother Fairy told her children. "But I am thankful you escaped without harm. I suppose Mr. Bullfrog was even more surprised than you!" She pulled them close and kissed each little fairy head. "I'll go with you in the morning to get your clothes," said Mother Fairy. "Just in case Mr. Bullfrog is waiting for your return."

At the brook the next day, the fairy boys plucked their little pants, clean and fresh, off the vine where they had left them. The fairy girls picked up their frocks and pulled them over their heads. But try as they might, the fairy children and their mother could not pull the girls' skirts loose from the vine. Twining tendrils had attached themselves tightly to the frilly skirts and refused to let go. Finally, at lunchtime, the vines released their grip and the skirts fell limp in the warm sun.

So if you look for the Morning Glory vine, go before the summer sun is mid-sky. Search along the water's edge for dainty little fairy skirts—pink, blue, white, and crimson—drying in the sunshine, but disappearing by afternoon when the fairies take them back.

joy fisher Hein

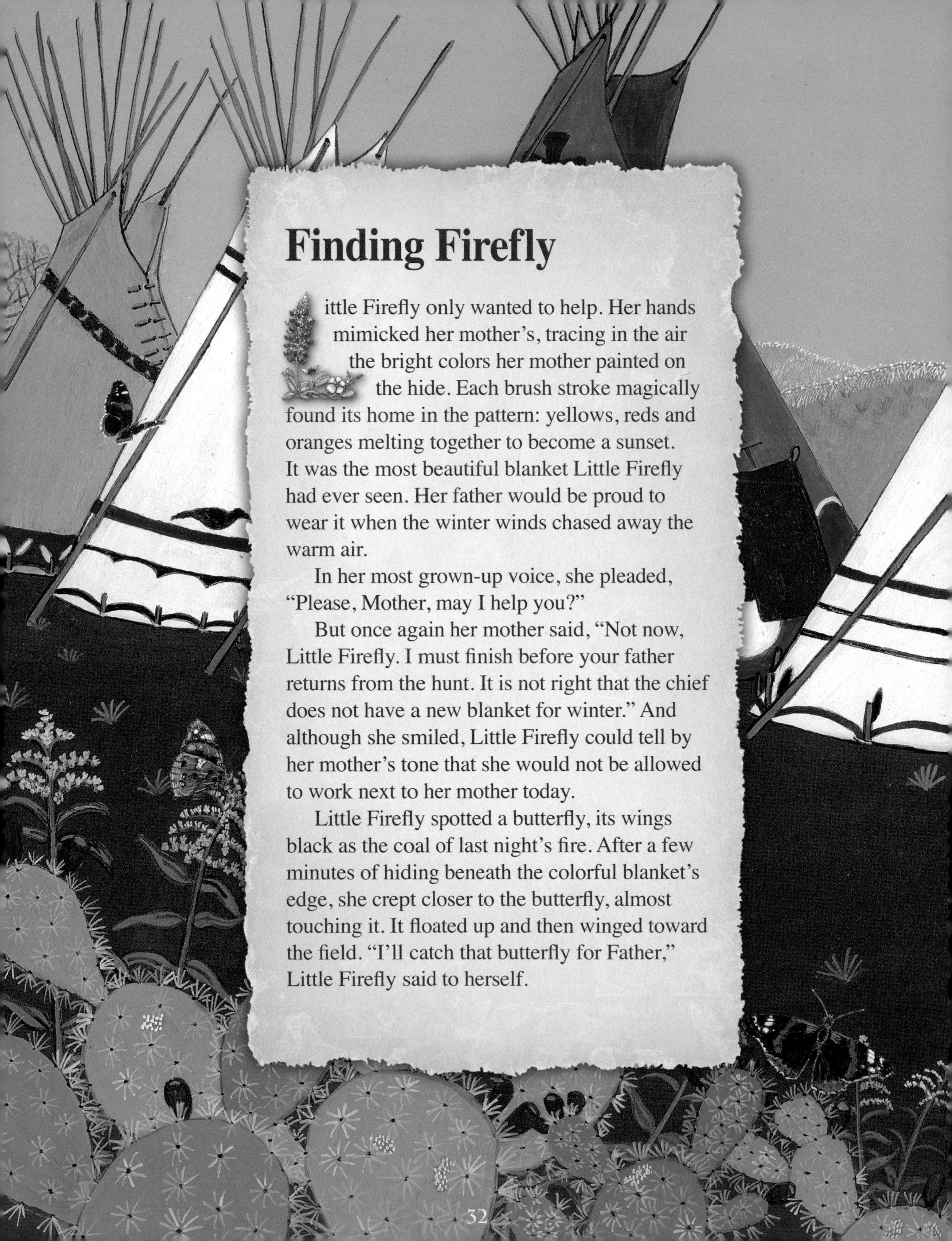

Finding Firefly

Little Firefly only wanted to help. Her hands mimicked her mother's, tracing in the air the bright colors her mother painted on the hide. Each brush stroke magically found its home in the pattern: yellows, reds and oranges melting together to become a sunset. It was the most beautiful blanket Little Firefly had ever seen. Her father would be proud to wear it when the winter winds chased away the warm air.

In her most grown-up voice, she pleaded, "Please, Mother, may I help you?"

But once again her mother said, "Not now, Little Firefly. I must finish before your father returns from the hunt. It is not right that the chief does not have a new blanket for winter." And although she smiled, Little Firefly could tell by her mother's tone that she would not be allowed to work next to her mother today.

Little Firefly spotted a butterfly, its wings black as the coal of last night's fire. After a few minutes of hiding beneath the colorful blanket's edge, she crept closer to the butterfly, almost touching it. It floated up and then winged toward the field. "I'll catch that butterfly for Father," Little Firefly said to herself.

Thinking of her father reminded her how much she wanted to go on the great hunt with him, but she dared not ask. That was not the way of her people. It had been difficult to hide her disappointment, watching her brothers leave with Father. And now Mother wanted to be left alone, too. So off Little Firefly ran, through the tall grass on a hunt of her own, chasing the butterfly that always seemed just beyond her fingers.

Running hard at first, then slowing to a walk, Little Firefly stalked her prey. It hovered low, going from flower to flower. Then, after darting ahead, it waited for her to catch up. The butterfly seemed to understand the game. It hovered above her head for a moment, then shot past her again, this time not pausing for Little Firefly. *That butterfly must be on its way back home to eat,* she thought. Her stomach rumbled, and she decided it was time for her to go home, too.

But when Little Firefly looked around her, she did not know which way to start.

The sun's warmth no longer touched her cheeks. Night crept toward the field. Where had the village gone? The tall grass that had been her friend before now swallowed up the clearing where her teepee stood. Racing to the edge of the meadow, she saw nothing familiar. An old tree looked at her angrily, the wind making its branches shake like fists, telling her she did not belong there. Night sounds sprang up quickly, closing in around her. A cricket rubbed its hind legs together, faster and faster, until the whirring noise hurt her ears. The darkness circled her.

Little Firefly looked around, feeling her stomach tighten, aching with fear instead of hunger. The more she searched, the more confused and scared she became. She crumpled to the ground and began to sob. Knowing her father was away on the hunt, she feared no one could find her. Cold and alone, she curled up, wishing for the warmth of the blanket her mother made. Then, as she had heard her father do, she prayed to the Great Spirit. While she prayed, the rhythmic noises of the night blended into a song that lulled her weary body to sleep.

She dreamed of her mother and the beautiful blanket she lovingly designed by blending the crimson, yellow and bright orange, just as the sun does in the twilight. A wonderful warmth settled across Little Firefly, and she slept soundly through the rest of the night.

"Little Firefly! Little Fi-i-i-r-fly-y-y-y-y-y!"

A voice called her name in the distance. Squinting in the bright morning sun, she stared down in astonishment. Covering her body was a blanket made of flowers. But they were flowers like she had never seen. Their ragged petals looked exactly like the blanket her mother painted. In the center of each bloom was a fiery orange cushion of tiny bristles.

The voice came closer and Little Firefly recognized her father's call. Jumping up and running to him, Little Firefly pulled her father to the spot where she had lain the night before. She told him how afraid and cold she had been. And then she told her father of her dream of the colorful blanket warming her, watching over her through the night, lying across her body just as the beautiful blanket of flowers lay across the field now.

The chief called to the Great Spirit at once. He thanked him for the protection the fuzzy-leafed plant had given his daughter. As the chief asked a blessing over the pinwheel flower, he and Little Firefly watched a sun yellow tip appear at the end of each reddish ray-petal.

So, look for that orangey bloom rising above the blades of grasses that transform into green each spring. As the days get longer and the nights begin to lose their chill, watch for a touch of bright yellow to appear on the edges of each flower. These are a promise of the sun's warmth and a sign of the chief's gratitude to the wildflower we call the Indian Blanket.

Magic Walking Stick

Long ago, the forest was so thick that the sun's light could not break through its cover. One late summer day, an old woman, bent and worn, wandered into the forest. She soon found herself deep in its heart. She walked for many hours, until, at last, she was nearly on the other side. As old people sometimes do, she grew tired. She knew she could not finish her journey without help.

"Mr. Tree, I have need of your aid," the old woman said. "Will you give me a small stick off your mighty branch so that I might have something to rest on as I walk?"

The great tree laughed at the woman. "You are old and ugly. I do not want the others to see you with one of *my* sticks. Go away, old woman, and come here no more."

The old woman walked a few more steps and looked up at another tree.

"Will you help me, Mr. Tree? You will soon loose your leaves to autumn's winds," the old woman said. "Please drop a small stick. I will bring it back when I am rested. No one will miss its shade come springtime."

"No!" the tree roared. The other trees will tease me for my soft heart. You are old and should not be walking alone anyway. You have caused your own misery. Go away, old woman, and bother me no more."

The old woman walked a bit further. She saw light pouring through the edge of the forest, but her strength was spent. She crumbled to the ground.

But the ground did not give her rest. A small stick poked her back. She rolled over and looked at the stick. It was crooked and had a knob near one end. She put her hand on the stick and rested her palm on the knob. It fit her hand perfectly! "Little Stick, will you help me? I must find my way out of the forest."

"Of course," said the little stick. "I am old and gnarled. I hoped to be chosen to make a child's swing, or a slingshot, or part of a tiny crib. But no one wants me. I am happy to be of use, my friend."

The old woman dug the stick into the ground and used it to push herself upright. With the stick's help, she finished her journey. As the pair came out from the forest, a curious thing happened. When the sunlight hit her, the old woman transformed into a shining fairy, as bright as the sun. Little Stick was amazed at her beauty.

"I am so grateful for your help, Little Stick," said the fairy. "What can I do to repay your kindness?"

Little Stick thought for a moment. He told the fairy that he had always desired to become part of a child's life. "But I've grown too old and brittle to be made into anything of use."

The beautiful fairy smiled. "You will be loved by *every* child!" From a tiny pouch at her waist, she pulled out a handful of golden dust and sprinkled it over Little Stick, turning him into a tall and elegant flower.

When you walk through the woods at the end of a late summer day, watch closely as you come to the forest's edge. That is where you can find the Goldenrod, his long plume of tiny yellow blooms shining in the sun's glow as he waits for the children who love him.

"Thomas? Child, come here," his mother called. Her red eyes filled with tears again. "We cannot stand idle. Go to our neighbors. Ask for food."

Thomas began the two-mile walk to their closest neighbors. He would ask if he could work to earn eggs and corn for his family. Da would not have taken without giving something in return. Neither would Thomas.

"I'm sorry, boy. We have nothin' to give ye," Mr. Cameron said. He put his big hand on Thomas' shoulder. The huge farmer looked away from the boy. "I am not sure how I can feed me own family."

Thomas could not bear to tell his mother there would be no help. The sun sank lower in the sky, his heart sinking with it. His pace slowed even more, each step sending a dirt cloud into the air. As he reached the top of the rise, he saw a glow beyond his house. It could not be the sunset. The sun was setting behind him. Orange and flickering, the bright light outlined the squatty mesquite trees between him and home. Suddenly a deer exploded from the thicket, her eyes wild with fear. As she fled, Thomas recognized the smell on her fur. It was fire. The prairie was on fire!

Thomas sprinted home, the energy of fear pushing his legs faster than he had ever run. Ma was gathering the girls and what belongings she could into their cart by the front porch. Thomas slipped past them, determined to get the one thing his father had left him—his tam. Throwing the hat onto his head, he grabbed the wagon's wooden tongue, meant for a mule, and tried to run with the cart. But before he had gone far down the trail, Thomas felt the wheels sink deep into the dry, loose dirt. "Grab Maggie, Ma! I'll carry Bonnie! Leave the rest!" Hearing the strong voice of her husband coming out of her son, his mother obeyed.

The flames grew around the edges, patches joining forces, merging into a single giant chasing the family with its hot breath. Mother and son moved in tandem, the silent girls in their arms lying wet and limp from the unrelenting heat.

"We'll never make it, Thomas."

"We have to, Ma! We've got to get to the old fort. Keep running!" cried Thomas.

The moments seemed like days as the duo surged ahead of the fire, only to let up and be outdistanced once again. They saw the white stone of the old fort ahead. It glowed eerily in the light of the approaching fire. Their neighbors, faces blackened with soot, ran out to them, grabbing the little girls and pushing the family into the fort's stacked-stone walls. They were safe! The soldiers had abandoned the fort decades ago, but it stood strong, solid against the fire's attack.

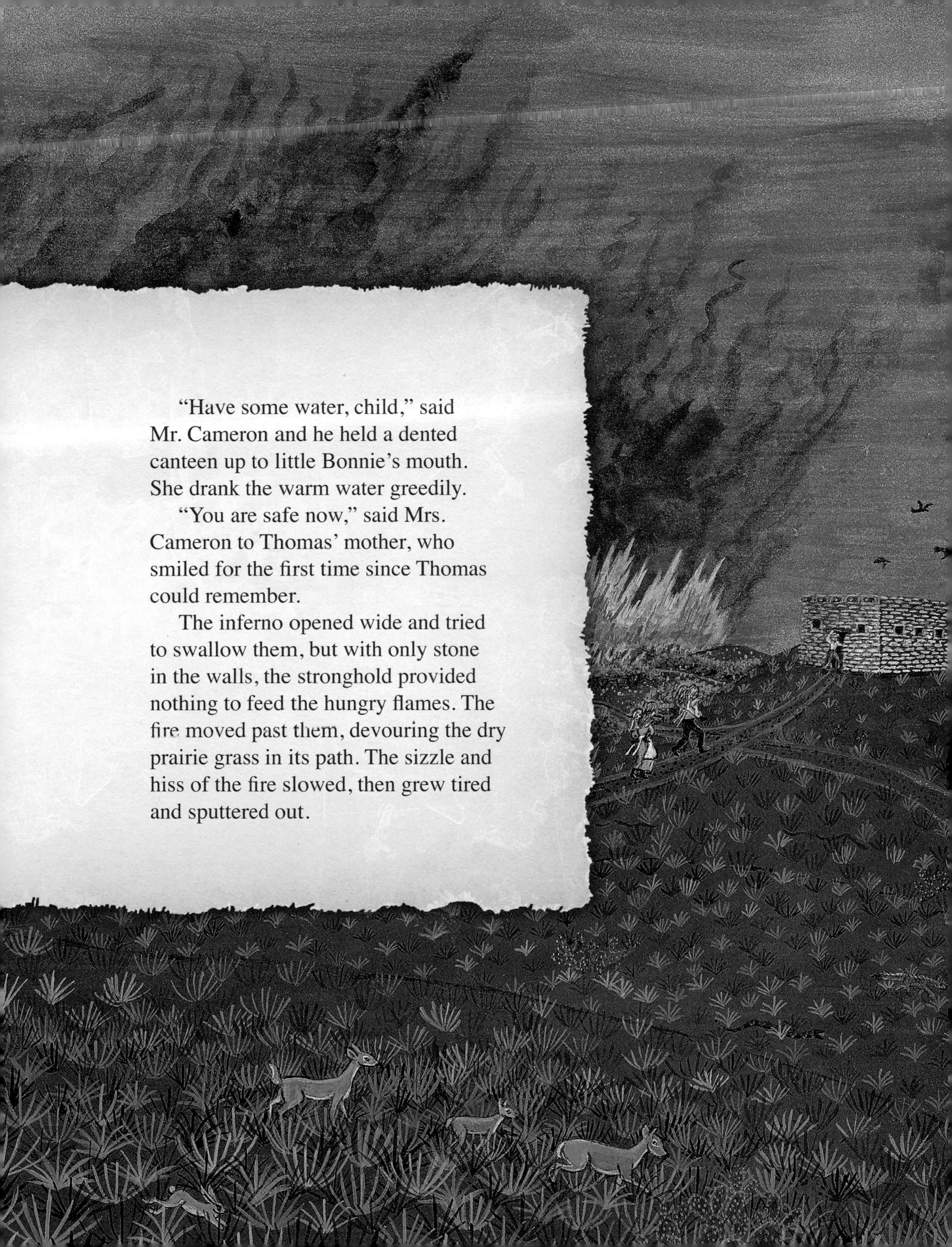

"Have some water, child," said Mr. Cameron and he held a dented canteen up to little Bonnie's mouth. She drank the warm water greedily.

"You are safe now," said Mrs. Cameron to Thomas' mother, who smiled for the first time since Thomas could remember.

The inferno opened wide and tried to swallow them, but with only stone in the walls, the stronghold provided nothing to feed the hungry flames. The fire moved past them, devouring the dry prairie grass in its path. The sizzle and hiss of the fire slowed, then grew tired and sputtered out.

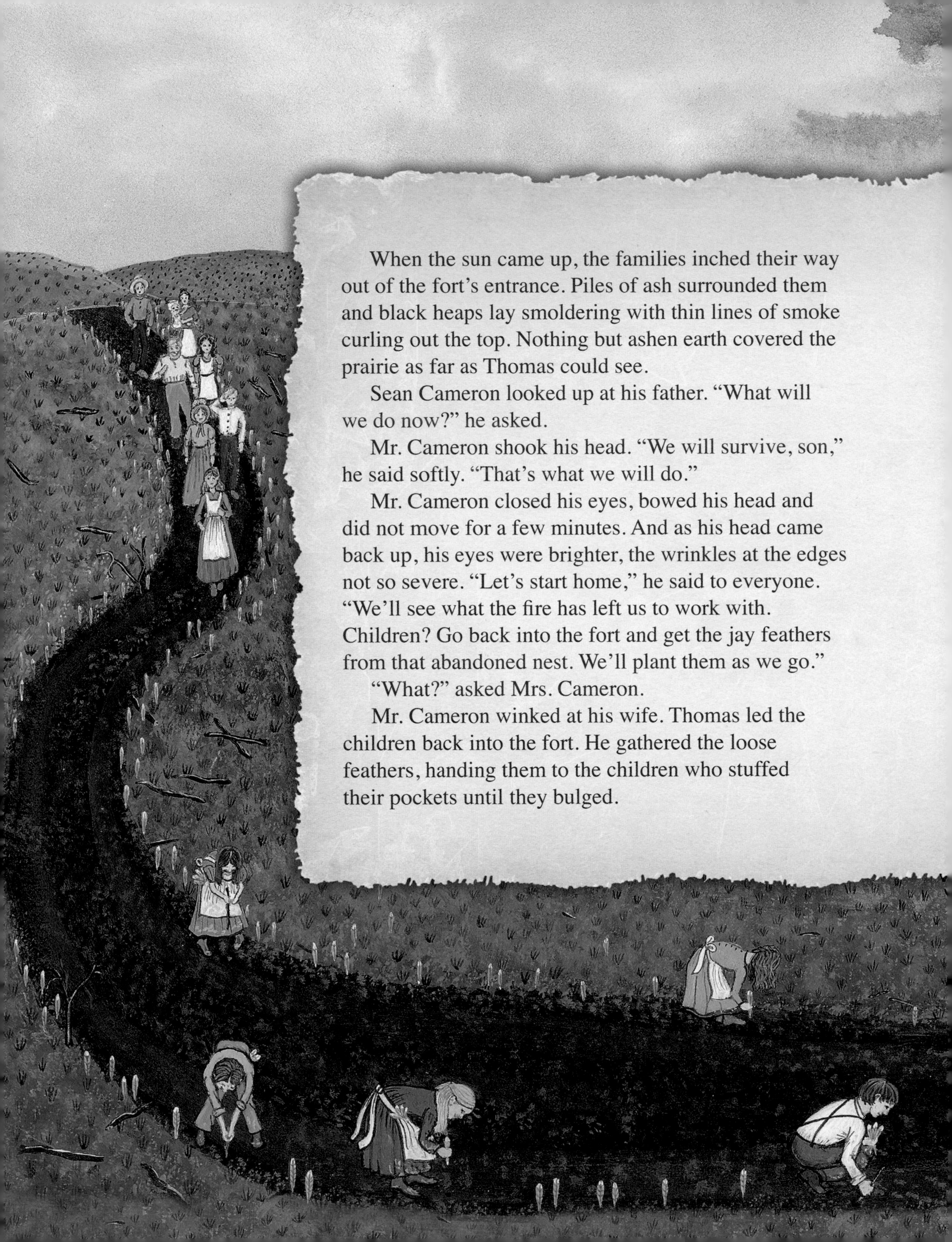

When the sun came up, the families inched their way out of the fort's entrance. Piles of ash surrounded them and black heaps lay smoldering with thin lines of smoke curling out the top. Nothing but ashen earth covered the prairie as far as Thomas could see.

Sean Cameron looked up at his father. "What will we do now?" he asked.

Mr. Cameron shook his head. "We will survive, son," he said softly. "That's what we will do."

Mr. Cameron closed his eyes, bowed his head and did not move for a few minutes. And as his head came back up, his eyes were brighter, the wrinkles at the edges not so severe. "Let's start home," he said to everyone. "We'll see what the fire has left us to work with. Children? Go back into the fort and get the jay feathers from that abandoned nest. We'll plant them as we go."

"What?" asked Mrs. Cameron.

Mr. Cameron winked at his wife. Thomas led the children back into the fort. He gathered the loose feathers, handing them to the children who stuffed their pockets until they bulged.

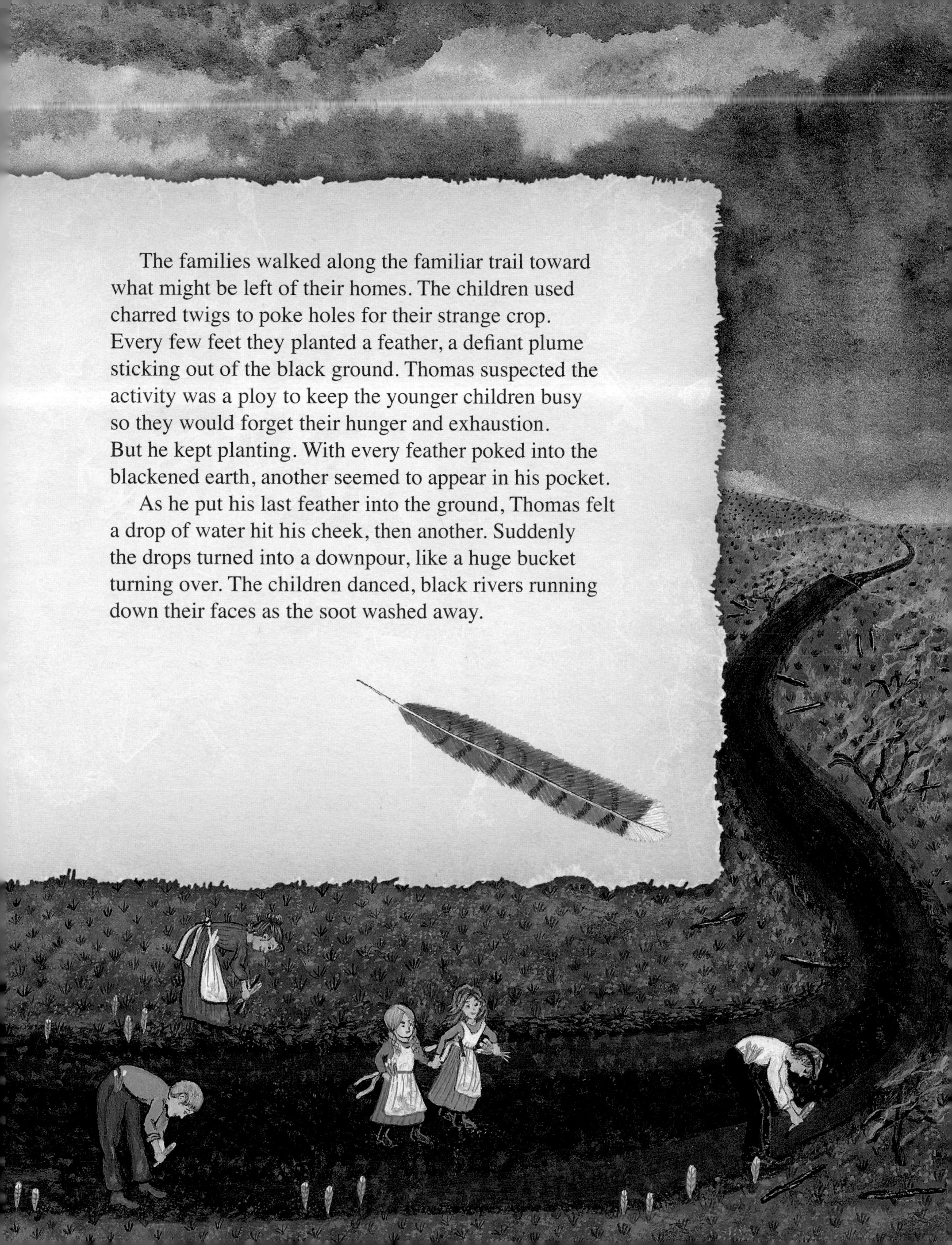

The families walked along the familiar trail toward what might be left of their homes. The children used charred twigs to poke holes for their strange crop. Every few feet they planted a feather, a defiant plume sticking out of the black ground. Thomas suspected the activity was a ploy to keep the younger children busy so they would forget their hunger and exhaustion. But he kept planting. With every feather poked into the blackened earth, another seemed to appear in his pocket.

As he put his last feather into the ground, Thomas felt a drop of water hit his cheek, then another. Suddenly the drops turned into a downpour, like a huge bucket turning over. The children danced, black rivers running down their faces as the soot washed away.

They opened their mouths wide to take big gulps of the cool water. Thomas looked around in amazement at how their world had changed. And then he saw it. The trees behind the group were scorched and still steaming, but the fields beside the trail were lush with the most beautiful blue flowers he had ever seen. They were the brightest blue: blue as the jay's feather, blue as Da's tam, his beloved blue bonnet.

"Look!" called Thomas, to the others. He pointed at the fields, no longer charred and burned. "The feathers have grown into blue bonnets!"

Each spring as the brown of winter is replaced with green, look through the grasses for leaves that stand open like a hand, waiting to catch the rains. When the spring rains come, a blue spike will shoot toward the heavens, reminding us of the blessing of life, and of Da's Bluebonnet.

FUN FACTS

Foxglove

- This plant is a virtual drugstore: early American settlers made a tea to soothe an upset stomach; Native Americans grind it for skin sores; and its cousin, *Digitalis purpurea*, is used by drug companies to make heart medicine.

- Dots on the petals of these flowers lead bees and other pollinators to the nectar. British children call them "poppers" because you can blow air into the bell shaped blooms and then pop them between your hands.

Water Lily

- Since it floats in water, this plant is also called "alligator bonnet." Its leaves—called "pads"—are notched on one edge and can be as large as a dinner plate.

- This flower is the emblem for the month of July. Although many Native Americans use it as food and tell of it in legends, Comanche stories most often speak of its beauty rather than its usefulness.

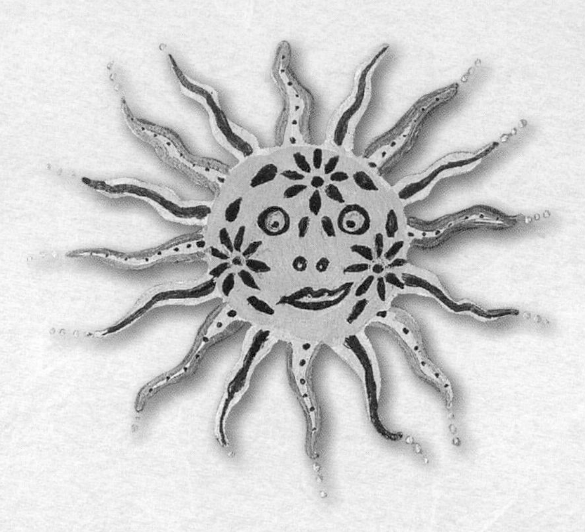

Prickly Pear Cactus

- Native Americans make candy from the fruit of this plant, called a "tuna," while the pads—sliced thin and cooked—are a favorite food called "nopalitos" by Spanish speaking cultures
- The Kiowa Indians made arrow tips for hunting out of the sharp spines of this plant and the Apache used them to tattoo their skin.

- This plant, which is the state plant of Texas, is home to cactus wrens, roadrunners and a tiny insect called the "cochineal mealy bug" that produces a valuable red dye that was used to make the red coats the British wore during the American Revolution.

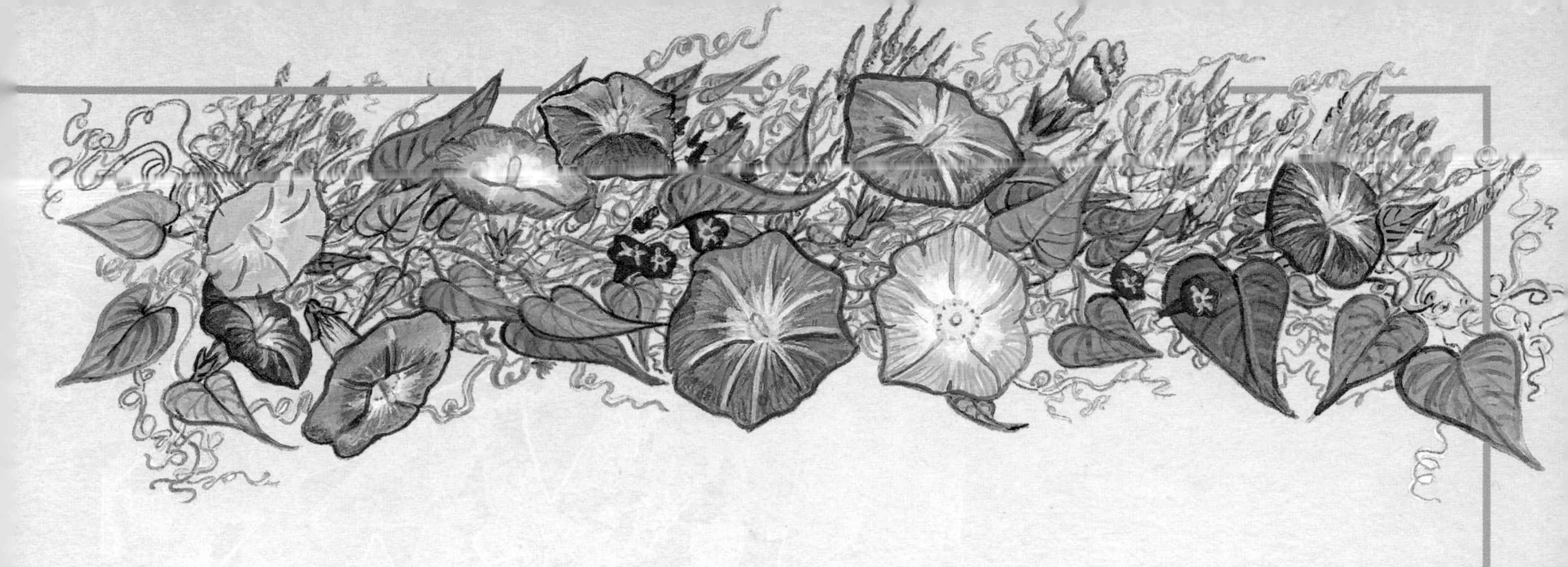

Morning Glory

- This plant family is considered by the Houma Indian of Louisiana to be a cure for snake-bites. One of its cousins—the wild potato vine—has a fleshy root like a potato that is roasted and eaten by many Native American tribes.
- This invasive climber will crawl over anything in its path if allowed. There are over 1000 different types of this plant around the world with various leaf shapes, all spouting a tubular flower that make them a favorite food of hummingbirds.

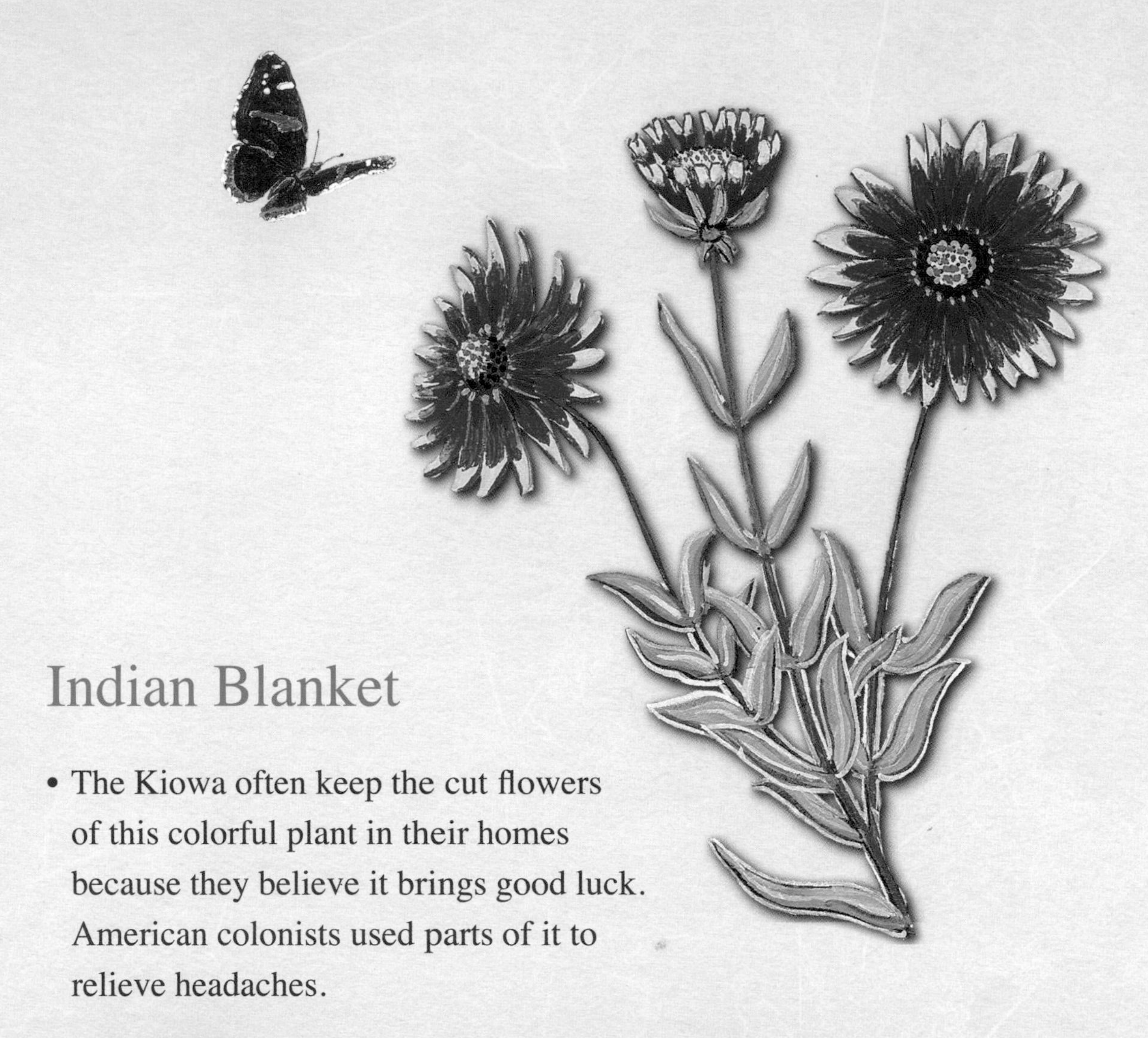

Indian Blanket

- The Kiowa often keep the cut flowers of this colorful plant in their homes because they believe it brings good luck. American colonists used parts of it to relieve headaches.

- Also called FIREWHEEL, this plant in the sunflower family thrives in dry conditions, partly because of its "hairy" stems and leaves that prevent water from evaporating from it.

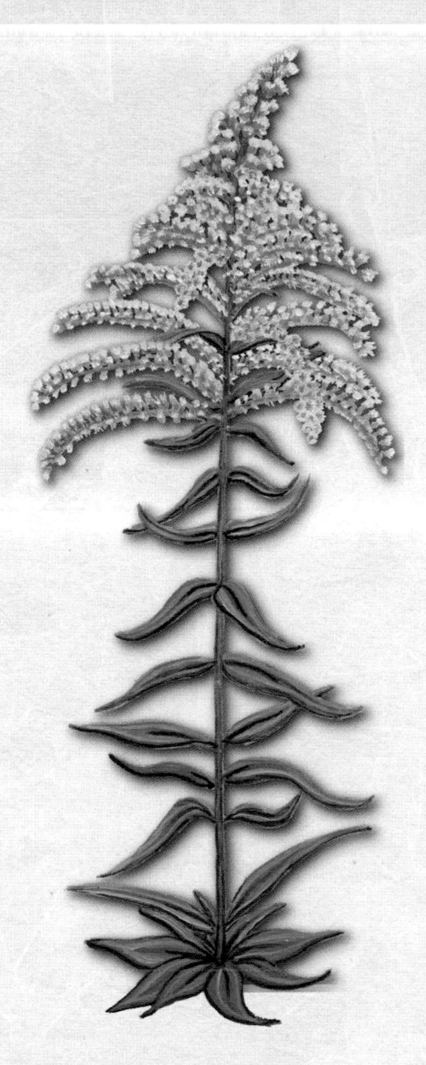

Goldenrod

- The Cherokee make tea out of this plant to help with digestion, and American colonists made "Liberty Tea" from it after dumping their English tea into the harbor during The Boston Tea Party. It is also the state flower of both Kentucky and Nebraska.
- Thomas Edison was able to extract latex from this plant and—with the help of Harvey Firestone—make a set of tires which Henry Ford used on his personal car.

Lupin

- Although its Latin family name means "the wolf" because it was thought the plant robbed the soil of nutrients, this plant actually enriches poor soil, releasing beneficial nitrogen that feeds other plants.
- The Texas bluebonnet is one of six different species of this plant in the state. All six are considered the state flower.

AFTERWORD

Folk tales, fairy tales, myths, legends: we use these terms interchangeably to describe a story that helps explain our world and how we fit in it. The account may be based on fact or be totally fictional. One story might tell how an object came to be. Another helps us see how something works. Yet another gives us insight into ourselves.

Bloomin' Tales came out of my desire to make it easier for children to recall the names of the plants around them. In my work designing educational gardens for schools, I find that when students hear how a plant got its name or the way early Texans used it, they remember not only the story but the plant as well. The legend connects the plant with the people, both in history and in the present. Myths tie us to inanimate objects in a personal way, uniting the many diverse pieces of our universe and presenting the world around us as an ordered, interdependent organism.

We live in an age that encourages us to focus on facts. But often today's facts are later proven fiction. While facts are important, without imagination, our greatest inventions and discoveries might not exist. The true Native Texans, now called Native Americans, are the only people indigenous to Texas. All other Texans came from somewhere else. Most of our state's wildflowers have beautiful Native American legends associated with them. Two of the legends included in this volume, "Starry Dreams" (WATER LILY, *Nymphaea ordorata*), and "Finding Firefly" (INDIAN BLANKET, *Gaillardia pulchella*), come from the oral tradition of the Native Texas people.

The other stories in this book arrived in Texas with the settlers who migrated to Texas came from many nations and every walk of life, most searching for political, financial or religious freedom. The immigrants' homeland marked them indelibly, so that they often preferred settling in a part of Texas that reminded them of the home they left. The security of familiar surroundings also helped them cope with difficult life on the Texas frontier. The English and French who left the lush green of their homelands headed to the rivers and forests of East Texas. The rocky hills of Central Texas attracted the German and Scottish migrants. South Texas felt like home to the Spanish missionaries and Mexican peoples, already accustomed to a hot, dry climate. Each of these groups brought memories of flowers they knew well from their childhood:

"Frolicking Fairies" (MORNING GLORY, *Convolvulus and Ipomoea* sp.) and "Bushy Fox's Tail" (FOXGLOVE, *Penstemon cobaea*) arrived with the English and French, fond of fairies and magic; "El Paisano and Señor Rattlesnake" (PRICKLY PEAR, *Opuntia engelmannii*), a Mexican story, brings alive the animal world of the desert and features a trickster; "The Magic Walking Stick" (GOLDENROD, *Solidago* sp.), is a colonial Texas story told by several ethnic groups; "When Feathers Bloomed" (BLUE-BONNET, *Lupinus* sp.), is a legend that refers to the Tam o'Shanter, a hat worn by Scottish settlers to Texas. The tam was named for a character in a Robert Burns poem and was originally always blue because that was the only available dye. Even the colorful plaid tams are often still referred to as "blue bonnets."

These legends are obviously not factual. Some come to us unchanged, even after being told for many generations. Others are based on actual incidents but grew more imaginative and unbelievable with each telling. They are *Texan*, after all! But in either case, I hope that, as you learn more about the great plants of Texas, you will discover more about the great people, too.

TEXAS MAP

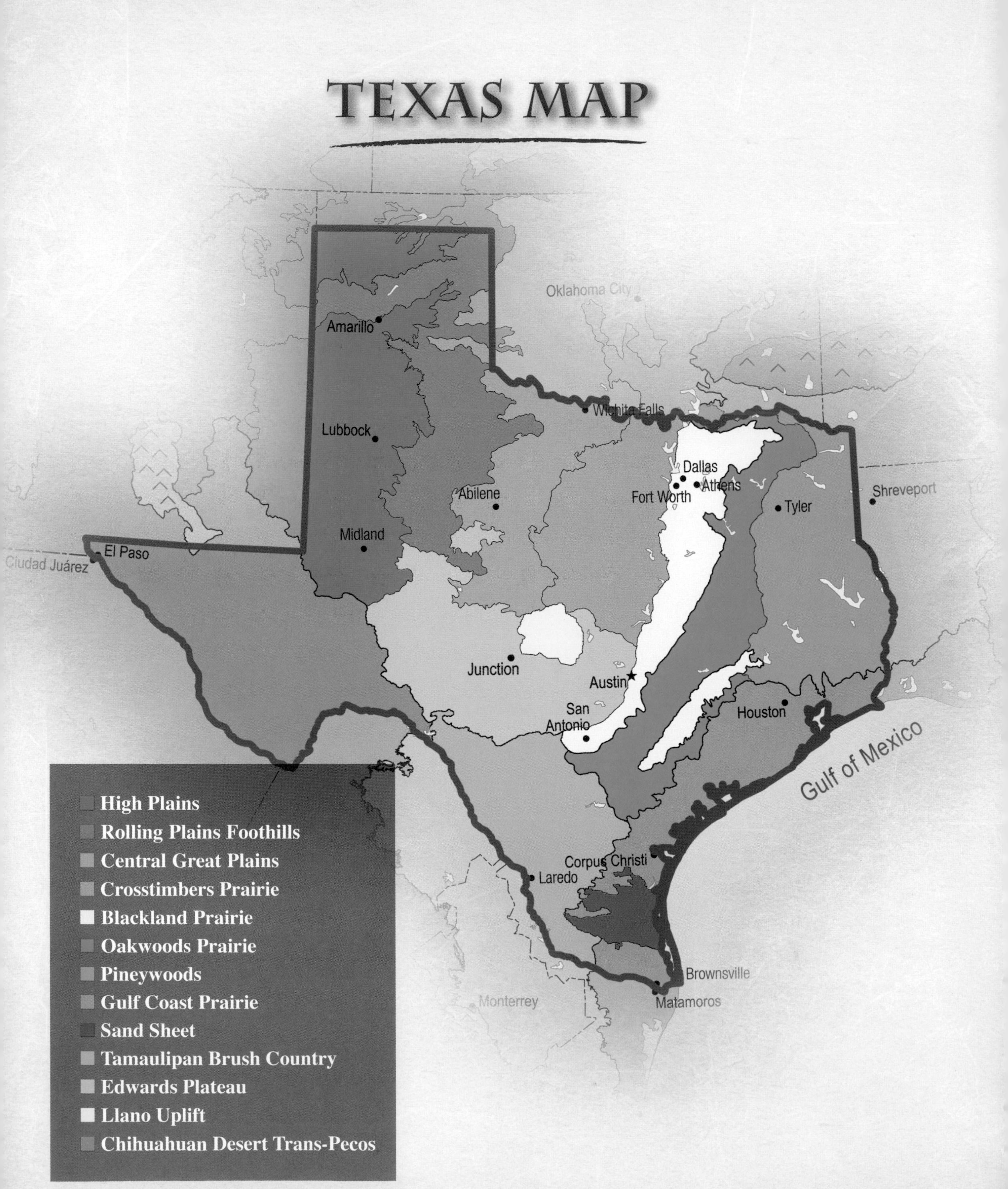
Oklahoma City
Amarillo
Lubbock
Wichita Falls
Dallas
Athens
Fort Worth
Shreveport
Tyler
Abilene
Midland
El Paso
Ciudad Juárez
Junction
Austin
San Antonio
Houston
Gulf of Mexico
Corpus Christi
Laredo
Brownsville
Monterrey
Matamoros
High Plains
Rolling Plains Foothills
Central Great Plains
Crosstimbers Prairie
Blackland Prairie
Oakwoods Prairie
Pineywoods
Gulf Coast Prairie
Sand Sheet
Tamaulipan Brush Country
Edwards Plateau
Llano Uplift
Chihuahuan Desert Trans-Pecos